F.W. - For my friends Lynn and David Bennett.
N.L. - For my nephew Tom.

First American edition published in 2000 by Carolrhoda Books, Inc.

Text copyright © 2000 by Frieda Wishinsky
Illustrations copyright © 2000 by Neal Layton

Published by arrangement with Bloomsbury Publishing Plc., London, England.

First Avenue Editions, an imprint of Lerner Publishing Group
241 First Avenue North, Minneapolis, MN 55401 U.S.A.

Website address: www.lernerbooks.com

Library of Congress Cataloging-in-Publication Data
Wishinsky, Frieda.
Nothing scares us / by Frieda Wishinsky ; illustrated by Neal Layton.—American ed.
p.   cm.
Summary: Best friends Lenny and Lucy each have a secret fear—Lucy is frightened by a TV monster, Lenny by spiders.
ISBN: 1–57505–669–0 (pbk.)
[1. Fear—Fiction. 2. Best friends—Fiction.] I. Layton, Neal, ill. II. Title.
PZ7.W78032 No 2000
[E]—dc21   00-008022

Printed and bound in Singapore by Tien Wah Press

2 3 4 5 6 7 – OS – 09 08 07 06 05 04

NOTHING SCARES US

by Frieda Wishinsky

illustrated by Neal Layton

CAROLRHODA BOOKS, INC., MINNEAPOLIS

Lucy and Lenny were best friends.
They did everything together.

They fought pirates in the playroom.

They chased aliens into the attic.

They tossed alligators out the window.

They threw monsters in the trash.

"We are the Fearless Two," sang Lenny.
"Nothing and no one scares us,"
sang Lucy.

Then one day Lenny turned on the TV. Three glaring eyes filled the screen. It was the CREATURE!

The CREATURE opened its slimy green mouth and sucked up a train.

"Neat!" said Lenny.

But Lucy said nothing.

"The CREATURE is on tomorrow!" said Lenny.
"I want to see it!"

But Lucy didn't.

That night Lucy saw the **CREATURE** at her window.
It opened its slimy mouth and roared.
Her window quivered like jelly.

Lucy dived under her covers.
She prayed the CREATURE would go away.
But it wouldn't.

Lucy tossed and turned. She peeked over her blanket.
The CREATURE was still there. Lucy was very tired.
"I'll think about something good," she thought.

She thought about butterflies and flowers. She thought about swimming in a blue lake and eating chocolate ice cream. She fell asleep.

In the morning, the CREATURE was gone.
Then Lenny called. "Come over!" said Lenny.
"The CREATURE is on at two."
Lucy's stomach started to hurt. She didn't want to see the CREATURE. But how could she tell Lenny?

What if he laughed? What if he called her a scaredy-cat?
What if he never played with her again?

Maybe she could say she was sick.
Maybe she could say her leg was broken.
Maybe she could say her stomach hurt.
But she couldn't. She had to go.

At two o'clock, Lucy's mother walked her to Lenny's.
"Hurry!" said Lenny. "The CREATURE'S starting."
And it was. The CREATURE was rising from the swamp.
Lenny smiled. Lucy's stomach twisted and knotted.
The CREATURE crawled out of the swamp. It crawled
toward a cottage, where a family was eating supper.

CHOP CHOP.

The CREATURE chopped the door down.
Lucy shut her eyes tight. She wanted to go home,
but before she could tell Lenny, someone screamed.

EEEEEEK!

Lucy popped her eyes open. The CREATURE was gone.
A man was talking about toothpaste.
Lucy turned to Lenny. But Lenny was gone.
There was nothing beside her but popcorn.

"Lenny!" called Lucy.

"Up here," said Lenny.
Lucy looked up. Lenny was standing on the couch.
"Look!" said Lenny, pointing to the popcorn bowl. A tiny black spider was crawling up the side.

"That?" said Lucy.
"Yes, that," said Lenny.
"It won't hurt you," said Lucy.
"Are you sure?" asked Lenny.
"I'm sure," said Lucy.

Lucy picked up the spider and dropped it out the window.
"Wow!" said Lenny. "You're so fearless. You're so brave."
"No, I'm not," said Lucy.
"You are to me," said Lenny. "I hate spiders."
"Well, I hate scary TV shows," said Lucy.
"You do?" asked Lenny. "Were you scared of
the CREATURE?"
"Yes," said Lucy.

Suddenly the TV rumbled. The CREATURE was back.
Lucy closed her eyes tight and covered her ears.
Lenny leaped from the couch and snapped off the TV.
"Thank you," said Lucy.

Lucy and Lenny cleaned up the popcorn. Then Lucy said,
"See the twelve-headed snake in the apple tree?"
"I see it," said Lenny.

"Let's get it," said Lucy.

Lucy threw Lenny his bow and arrow.
She slung hers over her shoulder. "Ready?" she asked.
"Ready," said Lenny.

Side by side, they marched to the tree.

"We are the Fearless Two,"
sang Lucy.

"Nothing and no one
scares us,"
sang Lenny.